Princess Josie

Written by
Lisa Paragary Engelken

Illustrations by
Karen Tarlton

Library of Congress Control Number: 2013951009
ISBN-13: 978-0-9891360-5-1
Princess Josie, Softcover Edition 2013
Printed in the United States of America

For more information about special discounts for bulk purchases, please contact 3L Publishing at 916.300.8012 or log onto our website at www.3LPublishing.com.
Illustrations by Karen Tarlton. Book design by Erin Pace-Molina.

Once upon a time
in a mystical land
far, far away,
there lived a special
princess.

Her name
was Princess Josie.

Princess Josie lived
in a beautiful castle
with other members
of her royal family:

the king, queen and
two princes.

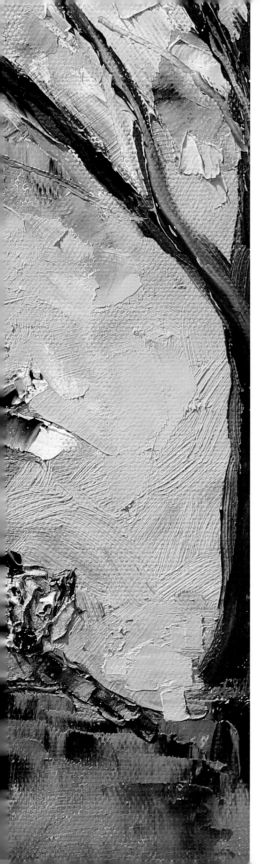

Princess Josie had very important jobs around the castle, like ridding the castle grounds of ferocious beasts.

She was also in
charge of keeping
intruders far away
from the castle door.

When the royal family would take excursions through the kingdom, Princess Josie would forge ahead to make sure that the area was secure.

She often had to
teach the princes
how to catch a ball.

She was even called
upon to provide
entertainment for
the royal family as a
beautiful dancer.

Yes, she could
even twirl like
a ballerina.

Josie's favorite time of the day was when the royal family would sit down for a grand feast where she was the guest of honor with her very special dining spot.

Her days were so
exhausting that she
would often take an
afternoon nap on her
royal bed so that she
would be refreshed
at night for her most
important job of all ...

keeping the princes
safe while they slept.

Good night
princes.

Good night
Princess Josie.

Author, *Lisa Paragary Engelken*, is a native Californian who graduated from UCLA in 1988 with a BA in English Literature. She currently resides in El Dorado Hills near Sacramento with her real life king, husband Pete and two princes, sons Matt and Jake. She is royally blessed to have Princess Josie as her daily companion and looks forward to their every adventure.